Bob the Builder™

Spud the Dragon

"Right, team, today we're working at Mrs Potts's house," said Bob, as he popped a roll of material into Muck's digger.

"Bob, what's that pink stuff?" Muck asked.

"It's insulating material for Mrs Potts's loft," explained Wendy. "It will stop the heat from escaping through the roof."

"**Can we fix it?**" asked Scoop.

"**Yes, we can!**" replied Muck and Dizzy.

"Er, yeah… I think so," said Lofty.

Over at the school, Spud was delivering a ladder to
Mrs Percival.

"Ah, thank you, Spud," she said. "This will come in handy for
the school play," and she dashed off to get everything ready.

On his way out of the school-yard, Spud noticed a pile of
dressing up clothes on a table.

"Ha ha! Look at all these goodies," he said,
as he grabbed an eye-patch and headscarf.

"Ahoy! Beware of
Spud the Pirate!
A-har!" he cried,
grabbing a cutlass
and swishing it around.

Then Spud spotted a hobby horse and cowboy hat on the table, and instantly changed into 'Spud the Lone Ranger'.

"Away...!" he shouted, as he galloped through the yard, bumping into a big, green costume.

"Cor! What's this?" he said, as he crawled inside, and became...

...Spud the Dragon!

"**Roarrrrr!**" cried Spud, as he raced away. "I'm sure Mrs Percival won't mind if I borrow this costume for a bit."

Spud the Dragon saw Muck on his way back to the yard.

"Hee hee! Time for some fun!" chuckled Spud.

"Wh-h-h-o are you?" stammered Muck.

"I'm a magic dragon," Spud answered. "I'll grant you a wish if you close your eyes."

So Muck closed his eyes and thought hard.

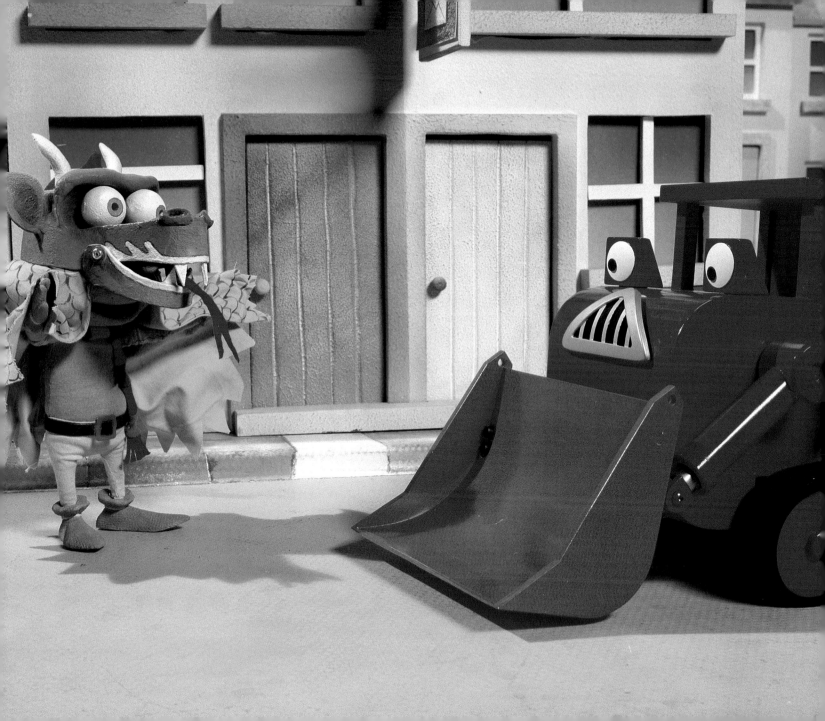

"I wish," said Muck, excitedly, "I wish I was twice as big as I am now, so that I could shift lots and lots of mud."

Spud was trying hard not to giggle as he drew a big black nose and whiskers on Muck's face, without him knowing.

"Mmm," continued Muck, "or how about...
I wish I wasn't ever scared of the dark..."

Spud added stripes to Muck's face, and some long cat's whiskers.

"Keep your eyes closed!" whispered Spud. And then he ran off!

"Hello?" said Muck. "Mr Dragon?" Muck opened his eyes slowly.

"He's vanished!" he gasped in amazement. "Wow! So he **was** magic after all. But where's my wish?"

He raced back to the yard to see if it was waiting for him there…

…But as soon as Muck arrived all the other machines burst out laughing.

"Erm… what's that on your face, Muck?" giggled Dizzy.

"What… what? Is it mud?" he asked.

"No! You've got a cat face!" chuckled Scoop.

"Wow! I wonder if this has got anything to do with the magic dragon?" Muck said. Dizzy, Scoop and Roley looked confused.

At Mrs Potts's house, Bob and Wendy were working in the loft. They'd found a lot of interesting things up there – clothes, toys and bits of material.

"Careful, Bob," said Wendy for the hundredth time. "You must stand on the wooden beams, or you'll..."

"**Aaargh!**" cried Bob, as his foot crashed through the floor.

"Oh dear!" exclaimed Mrs Potts. "Just look at my ceiling!"

"**Can we fix it?**" called Wendy.

"**Er... yes, we can!**" Bob replied in a quieter voice than usual.

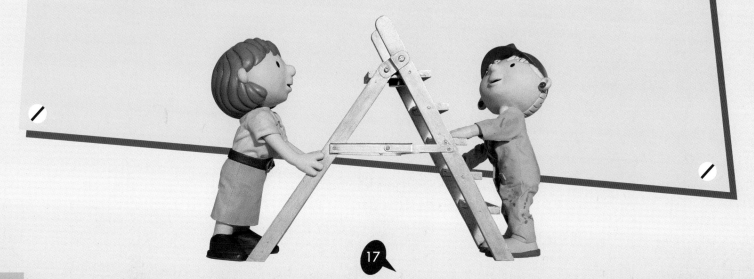

Wendy called outside for Lofty's help.

"We might need some extra paint and plaster," she said. "Could you pop back to the yard to get them, just in case?"

"Erm, OK Wendy," said Lofty. But as Lofty returned to the yard, he saw the most scary sight – a dragon with big googly eyes!

"**Roarrrr!**" growled Spud the Dragon.

"**Aaaarrrghhh!**" cried Lofty.

A scared Lofty raced back to Mrs Potts's house as fast as he possibly could.

Bob had managed to free his leg and was repairing the plasterboard in Mrs Potts's ceiling, and Wendy was in the loft laying down rolls of insulating material.

"There you are, Mrs Potts," said Bob, at last. "We're all done, and we didn't need that extra paint and plaster after all."

Just then, Lofty raced up.

"Oh, Wendy, oh, Bob!" he cried. "A... big... scary... dragon jumped out at me down the road!"

"Oh, Lofty!" said Wendy. "There aren't any dragons around here."

"There are... there is... I saw it," Lofty said. "It's got big googly eyes and everything!"

"It's all right," said Wendy. "Calm down. I'll tell you what, why don't Bob and I come with you and have a look?"

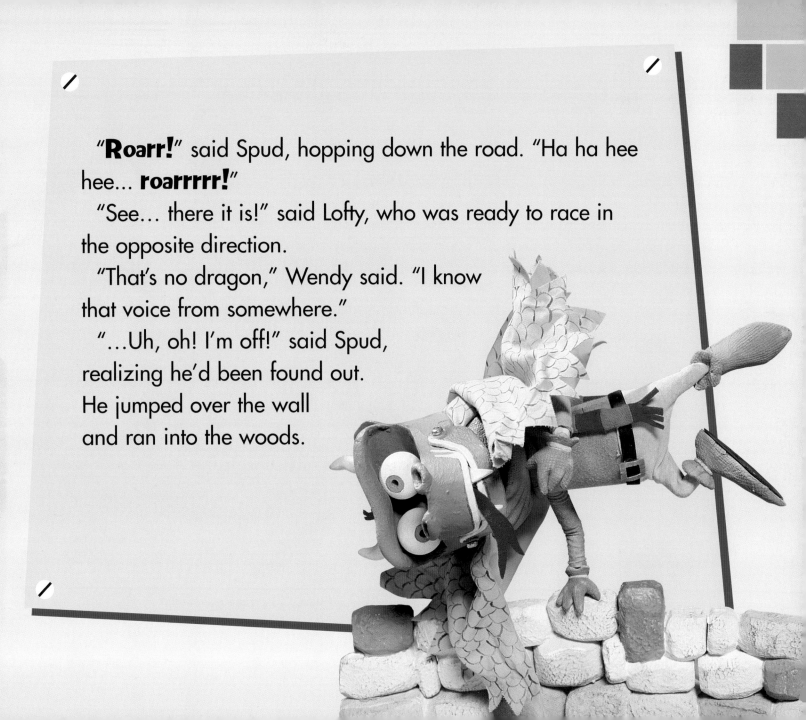

"**Roarr!**" said Spud, hopping down the road. "Ha ha hee hee... **roarrrrr!**"

"See... there it is!" said Lofty, who was ready to race in the opposite direction.

"That's no dragon," Wendy said. "I know that voice from somewhere."

"...Uh, oh! I'm off!" said Spud, realizing he'd been found out. He jumped over the wall and ran into the woods.

"Come on, after him!" called Wendy.

Bob and Wendy chased the dragon through the woods, leaping over logs and darting between tree trunks.

As the dragon ran, the branches ripped off more and more of the costume, until...

"**Woaaaahhh!**" cried the dragon as he tripped, and his mask flew off.

"Ah ha! I thought so," said Wendy. "It's Spud!"

Wendy, Spud and Bob went back to the school-yard to tell Mrs Percival what had happened.

"My dragon costume!" she said. "There's no time to fix it before the school play tonight."

"Oww, I'm really sorry, Mrs Percival," said Spud, hanging his head.

"Wait – I've got an idea!" said Wendy, and she dashed out of the school-yard.

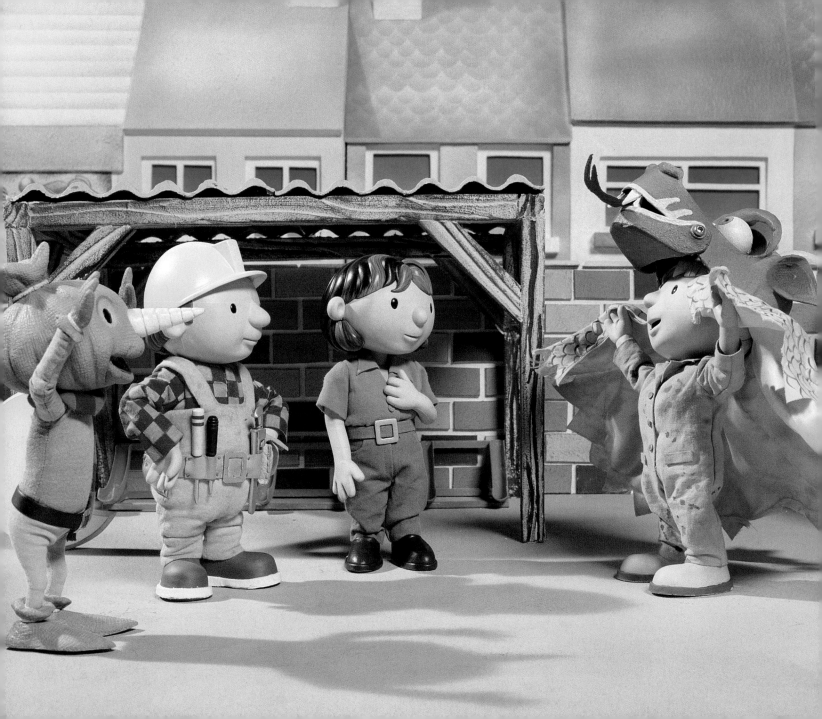

A while later…

"Hello, everyone!" roared a voice near the gate.

It was Wendy in the repaired dragon costume. She'd used some of the material in Mrs Potts's loft to mend the costume so it looked as good as new, and just as scary. So scary, in fact, that Spud took one look at it and screamed.

"**Argh! It's a real dragon!**" he cried, as he raced out of the yard.

"Come back, Spud!" called Wendy.

"Hide, everyone, hide!" screamed Spud, running off down the road. "Oh dear," said Wendy as she took off the mask. "It's only me, Spud!"

The End